A
Likely
Story

A Likely Story was first published in 1957.
It was collected in *The Stories of Mary Lavin II*, published in 1974,
reprinted here with permission of Constable Publishers.

Published by Poolbeg Press Ltd
123 Baldoyle Industrial Estate
Dublin 13, Ireland

This edition 1997

© Mary Lavin 1990

The moral right of the author has been asserted.

The Publishers gratefully acknowledge the support of
The Arts Council.

A catalogue record for this book is available from the British Library.

ISBN 1 85371 104 7

Illustrations by Alison Gault
Cover design by Poolbeg Group Services Ltd
Printed by The Guernsey Press Ltd,
Vale, Guernsey, Channel Islands.

A
Likely
Story

Mary Lavin

POOLBEG

nce upon a time there was a widow who had one son. He was her only son: her only joy. His name was Packy. Packy and the widow lived in a cottage in the shadow of the old abbey of Bective. The village of Bective was opposite, on the other side of the river Boyne.

Do you know Bective? Like a bird in the nest, it presses close to the soft green mound of the river bank, its handful of houses no more significant by day than the sheep that dot the far fields. But at night, when all its little lamps are lit, house by house, it is marked out on the hillside as clearly as the Great Bear is marked out in the sky. And on a still night it throws its shape in glitter on the water.

1

Many a time, when the widow lit her own lamp, Packy would go to the door, and stand on the threshold looking across the river at the lights on the other side, and at their reflection floating on the water, and it made him sigh to think that not a single spangle of that golden pattern was cast by their window panes. Too many thistles, and too many nettles, and too much rank untrodden grasses rose up in front of their cottage for its light ever to reach the water.

But the widow gave his sighs no hearing.

"It's bad enough to have one eyesore," she said, "without you wanting it doubled in the river!"

She was sorely ashamed of the cottage. When she was a bride, its walls were as white as the plumage of the swans that sailed below it on the Boyne, and its thatch struck a golden note in the green scene. But now its walls were a sorry colour; its thatch so rotten it had to be covered with sheets of iron, soon rusty as the docks that seeded up to the doorstep.

"If your father was alive he wouldn't have let the place get into this state," she told Packy every other day of his life. And this too made him sigh. It was a sad thing for a woman when there was no man about a house to keep it from falling down.

So, when the rain dinned on the tin roof, and the wind came through the broken panes, and when the smoke lost its foothold in the chimney and fell down again into the kitchen, like a sack of potatoes, he used to wish that he was a man. One day he threw his arms around his mother's middle.

"Don't you wish I was a man, Mother," he cried, "so I could fix up the cottage for you?"

But the widow gave him a curious look.

"I think I'd liefer have you the way you are, son," she said. She was so proud of him, every minute of the day, she couldn't imagine him being any better the next minute. He was a fine stump of a lad. He was as strong as a bush, and his eyes were as bright as the track of a snail. As for his cheeks, they were ruddy as the haws. And his hair had the same gloss as the gloss on the wing of a blackbird.

"Yes, I'd liefer have you the way you are, son," she said again, but she was pleased with him. She looked around at the smoky walls, and the broken panes stopped with old newspapers. "What would you do to it, I wonder—if you *were* a man?"

Her question put Packy at a bit of a loss.

Time and again he'd heard her say that all the money in the world wouldn't put the place to rights.

"Perhaps I'd build a new cottage!" he said cockily.

"What's that?" cried the widow. But she'd heard him all right, and she clapped her hands like a girl, and a glow came into her cheeks that you'd only expect to see in the cheeks of a girl. "I believe you would!" she cried, and she ran to the door and looked out. "Where would you build it, son? Up here on the hill, or down in the village? Would you have it thatched, or would you have it slated?"

"Slated, of course," said Packy decisively, "unless you'd prefer tiles?"

The widow looked at him in astonishment. Only the Council cottages had tiles.

"Would there be much of a differ in the price?" she asked timidly.

"Tiles would cost a bit more I think," Packy hazarded. "And they mightn't be worth the differ."

A shadow fell on the widow's joy.

"Ah well," she said. "No matter! If we couldn't do everything well I'd just as soon not build at all! I wouldn't want to give it to say that it was a shoddy job."

There would be nothing shoddy about it though.

"I was only thinking," said Packy, "that it might be better to put the money into comfort than into show. We might get a range in the kitchen for what we'd save on the tiles."

"A range?" cried the widow. Never, never, would she have presumed to think that she, who had stooped over a hob for forty years, would ever have a big back range to stand in front of and poke with a poker. But all the same she felt that it might be as well not to let Packy see she was surprised. Better to let him think she took a range for granted. So instead of showing surprise she looked at him slyly out of the corner of her eye. "What about a pump?" she said. "A pump in the yard?" But she saw at once by the way his face fell that she'd gone a bit too far. The Council houses hadn't as much as a mention of a pump.

"I thought maybe it would be good enough if we built near the pump in the village," Packy said uneasily.

"Sure of course it would be good enough, son," she conceded quickly. After all, a pump in the yard was only a dream within a dream. But she would have given a lot to stand at the window and see her neighbours passing on their way to the pump in the village, and better still to see them passing back again, their arms dragging out of them with the weight of the bucket, while all she'd have to do would be to walk out into her own yard for a little tinful any time she wanted. It would make up for all the hardship she'd ever suffered. Oh, she'd give a lot to have a pump in her own yard!

And looking at her face, Packy would have given a lot to gratify her with a pump.

"I wonder would it cost a lot of money?" he asked.

"Ah, I'm afraid it would, son," said the widow, dolefully. Then all at once she clapped her hands. "What about the money we'll get for this place when the new cottage is built? Couldn't we use that money to put down a pump?"

Packy stared blankly at her. Up to that moment he had altogether forgotten that building a new cottage would mean leaving the old one. To him, the little cottage never seemed as bad as it did to the widow. He had listened, it is true, to her daily litany of its defects, but out of politeness only. Never had he seen it with her eyes, but always with his own. According to her, its tin roof was an eyesore, but he liked to hear the raindrops falling on it clear and sweet. According to her, the windows were too low, and they didn't let in enough light by day, but in bed at night he could stare straight up at the stars without raising his head from the pillow. And that was a great thing surely! According to her, the cow shed was too close to the house, but if he woke in the middle of the night, he liked to hear Bessie, the old cow, pulling at her tyings, and on cold winter nights it comforted him to find that the fierce night air was not strong enough to kill the warm smell that came from her byre.

There was one wintry night and he thought he'd die before morning, like the poor thrushes that at times fell down out of the air, too stiff to fly, but when he thought of Bessie and the way the old cow's breath kept the byre warm, he cupped his own two hands around his mouth and breathed into them, and soon he too began to feel warm and comfortable. To him, that night it seemed that together, he and the old cow, with their living breath were stronger than their enemies, the elements. Oh, say what you liked, a cow was great company. And as far as he was concerned, the nearer she was to the house the better. So too with many other things that the widow thought were faults in the little house; as often as not to Packy they were things in its favour. Indeed, it would want to be a wonderful place that would seem nicer and homelier to him than the cottage where he was born. After all, his Mother came to it only by chance, but he came to it as a snail comes to its shell.

"Oh, Mother!" he cried, "maybe we oughtn't to part with the old cottage till we see first if we're going to like the new one."

To hear the sad note in his voice you'd think the day of the flitting was upon them. The widow had to laugh.

"Is that the way with you, son? You're getting sorry you made such big promises! Ah, never mind. It'll be a long time yet before you're fit to build a house for any woman, and when that time does come, I don't suppose it will be for your old mother you'll be building it."

But her meaning was so lost on him.

"And for who else?" he cried.

But the widow turned away and as she did she caught sight of the clock.

"Look at the time! You're going to be late for school. And I have to cut your lunch yet," she said crossly. Bustling up from the bench she seized the big cake of soda bread that she had baked and set to cool on the kitchen window-sill before he was out of bed that morning.

"Will this be enough for you?" she cried, cleaving the knife down through the bread and mortaring together two big slices with a slab of yellow butter. Then, as he stuffed the bread into his satchel and ran out of the door, she ran after him. "Hurry home, son," she called out, leaning far over the gate to watch him go up the road.

Hardly ever did he go out of the house that she didn't watch him out of sight, and hardly ever did he come home that she wasn't there again, waiting to get the first glimpse of him. And all the time between his going and his coming, her heart was in her mouth wondering if he was safe and sound. For this reason she was often a bit edgy with him when he did come home, especially if he was a few minutes late as he was sometimes when he fell in with his friends, the Tubridys.

The widow was death on the Tubridys, although nobody, least of all herself, could say why this should be so. Perhaps it was that, although she often said the whole three Tubridys—Christy and Donny and poor little

Marty—all sewn up together wouldn't put a patch on her Packy, still—maybe—it annoyed her to see them trotting along behind Rose Tubridy on the way to Mass of a Sunday while she had only the one set of feet running to keep up with her.

"Well! What nonsense did the Tubridys put into your head today?" she'd call out as soon as he came within earshot.

"Oh, wait till you hear, Mother!" he'd cry, and before he got to the gate at all, he'd begin to tell all he heard that day.

One day he was very excited.

"What do you know, Mother! There is a big pot of gold buried beyond in the old abbey! Christy Tubridy is after telling me about it. He didn't know anything about it either until last night when his father told him while they were all sitting around the fire. He said he'd have got it himself long ago, only every time he put the spade into the ground, a big white cock appeared on the top of the old abbey and flapped its wings at him, and crowed three times! He had to let go the spade and run for his life! What do you think of that, Mother?"

But the widow didn't give him much hearing.

"A likely story!" she said. "What harm

would an innocent old cock have done him? Him of all people: that ought to be well used to the sound of cocks and hens, with the dungheap right under the window of the house. It's a wonder he wasn't deafened long ago with cocks crowing right into his ear. Oh, it would take more than an old cock to scare that man. And furthermore, let me tell you that if there was something to be got for nothing in this world, the devil himself wouldn't knock a feather out of him till he got it. You mark my words, son, if there was as much as a farthing buried in the old abbey, by now old Tubridy would have scratched up the whole place looking for it. He wouldn't have left one stone standing on another. He'd have done a better job on it than Cromwell! A pot of gold, indeed! A likely story!"

"I suppose you're right," said Packy, and he left down the spade that he had grabbed up to go digging for the gold.

"Don't be so ready to believe everything you hear!" said his mother.

But barely a day later he came running home again to tell something else he had heard.

"Mother! Mother! Do you know the heap of old stones at the bottom of the hill in Claddy graveyard, where there was an old church one time? Well, last night Christy Tubridy's father told him that when they were building that church long ago they never meant to build it there at all, but at the top of the hill, only the morning after they brought up the first load of stones and gravel, where did they find it all but down at the bottom of the hill. Nobody knew how it got there, but they had to spend the day bringing it all up again. And what do you suppose? The morning after when they came to work, there were all the stones and the gravel down at the bottom once more. And the same thing happened the day after that again and on every day after for seven days. But on the seventh day they knew that it must be the work of the Shee. The Shee didn't want a church built on that hill at all. There was no use going against them, so they built it down in the hollow."

But the widow didn't give him any hearing this time either.

"A likely story!" she said. "It's my opinion that the workmen that carried those stones up the hill by day, were the same that carried them down-hill at night. I don't suppose the men that were going in those days liked work any better than the men that are going nowadays, and it's likely they decided it would pay them better to put in a few hours overtime taking down the stones, than be lugging them up there for an eternity—as they would be in those days with not many implements. The Shee indeed! How well no one thought of sitting up one night to see who was doing the good work? Oh no. Well they knew it wasn't the Shee! But it suited them to let on to it. The Shee indeed! If that hill belongs to the Shee—which I very much doubt—what harm would it do them to have a church built on it? Isn't it *inside* the hills the Shee live? What do they care what happens outside on the hillside? A likely story! I wonder when are you going to stop heeding those Tubridys and their nonsense?"

Never, it seemed, for the very next day he came running down the road as if he'd never get inside the gate quick enough to tell another story.

"Oh Mother!" he cried, jumping across the puddles at the door. "Are you sure I'm yours? I mean, are you sure that I belong to you— that I'm not a changeling? Because Christy Tubridy told me that their Marty is one. I always thought he was their real brother, didn't you? Well, he's not. One day, when he was a baby, their mother was hanging out the clothes to dry on the bushes, and she had him in a basket on the ground beside her, but when she was finished hanging up the clothes she looked into the basket, and it wasn't her own baby at all that was in it but another one altogether that she'd never seen before, all wizened up, with a cute little face on him like a little old man. It was the Shee that came and stole her baby, and put the other crabby fellow in place of him. The Tubridys were terribly annoyed, but they couldn't do anything about it, and they had to rear up Marty like he was their own."

But this time the widow gave him no hearing at all.

"A likely story!" she cried. "A likely story indeed. Oh, isn't it remarkable the lengths people will go to to make excuses for themselves. That poor child, Marty Tubridy, was never anything but a crabby thing. He's a Tubridy, all right. Isn't he the dead spit of his old grandfather that's only dead this ten years? I remember him well. So they want to let on he's a changeling? God give them wit. The Shee indeed! The Shee are no more ready than any other kind of people to do themselves a bad turn, and if they make it a

habit to steal human children—which I very
much doubt—I'd say they'd be on the watch
for some child a bit better favoured than one
of those poor Tubridys. Now, if it was *you* they
put their eye on, son, that would be a
different matter, because—even if it's me that
says it—you were the sonsiest baby anyone
ever saw. Not indeed that I ever left you lying
about in a basket under the bushes. It would
want to be someone smart that would have
stolen you. I never once took my eyes off you
from the first minute I clapped them on to
you, till you were big enough to look after
yourself—which I suppose you are now? Or
are you? Sometimes I doubt it when you
come home to me stuffed with nonsense.
Changeling indeed. A likely story!"

But as a matter of fact it would have been
hard to find a story that would not be a likely
story to the widow. The gusts of her wisdom
blew so fiercely about the cottage that after a
while Packy began to feel that it wasn't worth
while opening his own mouth at all, so
quickly did his mother rend his words into
rags. And when, one spring, he began to fancy
every time he went out of doors that there
was someone beckoning to him, and calling
him by name, he said nothing at all about it

to his mother. For of course he could be mistaken. It was mostly in the evenings that the fancies came to him, and the mist that rose up from the river and wandered over the fields often took odd shapes. There were even days when it never wholly lifted, and like bits of white wool torn from the backs of the sheep as they scrambled through briars and bushes, or rubbed up against barbed wire, the mist lay about the ground in unexpected hollows. It lay in the hollows that are to be found in old pasture that once was broken by the plough, and on the shallow ridges where the fallow meets the ley. Ah yes. It was easy enough then to mistake it for a white hand lifted, or a face turned for an instant towards you, and then turned swiftly aside.

It is said however that a person will get used to anything, and after a while Packy got used to his fancies. He got used to them, but he was less eager than usual to go out and wander in the fields and woods, above all after the sun went below the tops of the trees. And the widow soon noticed this. It wasn't like him to hang about the cottage after school.

What was the matter, she wondered? Did something ail him?

"Where are the Tubridys these days, son?" she asked at last. "God knows they're here often enough when they're not wanted. It's a wonder you wouldn't like to go off with them for a ramble in the woods."

She went to the door and looked out. It was the month of May, the very first day of it. But Packy didn't stir from the fire. Nor the next day either. Nor the next. Nor the next.

"That fire won't burn any brighter for you to be hatching it," said the widow at last.

That was true, thought Packy, for it was a poor fire surely. He looked at it with remorse. It was nearly out. There was nothing on the hearth but a handful of twigs that were more like the makings of a jackdaw's nest than the making of a fire. It was like a tinker's fire, no sooner kindled than crackled away in a shower of sparks. He looked at his mother. He knew what was wrong. She had no one to depend on for firing now that he never went out, for, in the past, he had never come back without a big armful of branches from the neighbouring demesne. He looked at her hands. They were all scratched and scored from plucking the bushes.

"Oh, Mother," he cried in true contrition, "tomorrow on my way home from school I'll go into the woods, no matter what, and get you an armful of branches!"

But the next day—and in broad sunlight too—his fancies were worse than ever.

Just as the bell rang to call in the scholars from play, what did Packy see, around the corner of the schoolhouse, but a finger beckoning: beckoning to him. It turned out to be only the flickering of a shadow cast on the wall by an old hawthorn tree beyond the gable, but all the same it unsettled him. And when school was over he made sure to keep in the middle of the little drove of scholars that went his way home.

For there is no loneliness like the loneliness of the roads of Meath, with the big, high hedges rising up to either side of you, so that you can't even see the cattle in the fields, but only hear them inside wading in the deep grass and pulling at the brittle young briars in the hedge. Closed in between those high hedges, the road often seems endless to those who trudge along it, up hill and down, for although to the men who make ordnance maps the undulations of the land may seem no greater than the gentle undulations of the birds rising and dipping in the air above it, yet to those who go always on foot—the herd after his flock, the scholar with his satchel on his back—it has as many ripples as a sheet in the wind, and not only that, but it often seems to ripple in such a way that the rises are always in front, and the dips always behind.

It was that way with Packy anyway.

Oh, how good it would be at home: first to catch a glimpse of the little rusty roof, and then to run in at the gate and feel the splatters of the mud on his knees as he'd dash through the puddles in front of the door.

It was not till he got to Connells Cross that he remembered his promise about the firewood. Oh sorely, sorely was he tempted to break that promise, but after one last look at the far tin roof that had just come into view above the hedge he let the little flock of scholars go forward without him. Then, with a sad look after them he climbed up on the wall of the demesne and jumped down on the other side. Immediately, under his feet twigs and branches cracked like glass, and for a minute he was tempted to gather an armful although he knew well they were only larch and pine. But he put the base temptation from him. Try to light a fire with larch? Wasn't it larch carpenters put in the stairs of

a house so the people could get down it safely
if the house took fire. And pine? Wasn't it a
dangerous timber always spitting out sparks
that would burn holes the size of buttons in
the leg of your trousers. Oh no; he'd have to
do better than that; he'd have to get beech or
ash or sycamore or oak. And to get them he'd
have to go deep into the woods to where the
trees were as old as the Christian world. He'd
have to go as far as the little cemetery of
Claddy. There, among the tottering tomb-
stones and the fallen masonry of the ancient
church, there was always a litter of dead
branches, and what was more, every branch
was crotched over with grey lichen to make it
easier to see against the dark mould of the
earth.

Like all cemeteries, the cemetery of Claddy
was a lonely place, and to get to it he would
have to cross the hill that Christy Tubridy
said belonged to the Shee, but he remembered
that his mother had heaped scorn on that
kind of talk. All the same, when Packy came
to the small pathway that led up to the hill,
he faltered because it was so overgrown with
laurel it was more like a tunnel than a path.
Away at the far end of the tunnel, though,
there was a glade and there the light lay

white and beautiful on the bark of the trees. Shutting his eyes, Packy dashed into the leafy tunnel and didn't open them until he was out of it. But when he did open them he had to blink, because, just as the sky would soon sparkle with stars, so, everywhere, under his feet the dark earth sparkled with white windflowers. Who could be afraid in such a place?

As for the branches: the ground was strewn with them. Ah! there was a good one. There was a fine dry one. And there was one would burn for an hour.

But it didn't pay to be too hasty. That last was a branch of blackthorn and it gave him a nasty prick— "Ouch," it hurt. Letting fall his bundle, Packy stuck his finger into his mouth, but the thorn had gone deep and he couldn't suck it out. He'd have to stoup his finger in hot water, or get his mother to put a poultice of bread and water on it. He'd better not forget either, he told himself, because there was poison in thorns. Christy Tubridy knew a man who . . . At the thought of the Tubridys, though, Packy grew uneasy. All the stories they had ever told him again crowded back into his mind. Supposing those stories were true? Supposing the Shee really did still wander about the world? Supposing they did steal away human children?

Suddenly his heart began to beat so fast it felt like it was only inside his shirt it was instead of inside his skin. And the next minute, leaving his bundle of twigs where it lay, he made for the green pathway up which he had come, meaning to fling himself down it as if it were a hole in the ground.

And that is what he would have done only that—right beside him—sitting on the stump of a tree, he caught sight of a little man. He was well dressed—a gentleman from the Big House, perhaps? Now although Packy was glad he was not alone, he was afraid the gentleman might be cross with him for trespassing. But not at all. The gentleman was very affable.

"There's a fine dry limb of a tree," he said, pointing to a bough of ash that Packy had overlooked.

He spoke so civilly that Packy ventured a close look at him.

Was he a man at all, he wondered? The clothes on him were as fine as silk, and a most surprising colour: green. As for his shoes, they were so fine his muscles rippled under the leather like the muscles of a finely bred horse ripple under his skin. There was something a bit odd about him.

"Thank you, sir," said Packy cautiously and he bent and picked up the branch.

"Don't mention it: I assure you it's a pleasure to assist you, Packy." In surprise Packy stared. The gentleman knew his name!

"Yes, Packy, I know your name—and all about you," he said, smiling. "In fact I have been endeavouring all the week to have a word with you—alone, that is to say—but I found it impossible to attract your attention—until now."

Packy started. So he wasn't mistaken after all when he fancied that someone was beckoning to him, and raising a hand.

"Was it you, sir?" he cried in amazement. "I thought it was only the mist. Tell me, sir—were you at it again today? You were. Well doesn't that beat all!" said Packy. "I thought it was a branch of hawthorn swaying in the wind."

The little gentleman bowed.

"I'm complimented. A beautiful tree; always a favourite of mine, especially a lone bush of it in the middle of a green field. But to come to practical matters. I suppose you're wondering what I wanted to see you about.

Well, let me tell you straight away—I understand that you are dissatisfied with the condition of your cottage—is that so?"

He was a County Councillor. That was it!—thought Packy. He'd come to make a report on the condition of the cottage. And to think that he had nearly run away from him.

"It's in a very bad state, sir," he said. "My mother is very anxious to get out of it."

To a County Councillor that ought to be broad enough! Better however leave nothing to chance. "Perhaps there is something you could do for us, sir," he said. Throwing down his bundle of kindling he went nearer. What were a few bits of rotten branch to compare with the news he'd be bringing home if the Councillor promised him a Council cottage?

"Well, Packy, perhaps there may be something I can do for you," said the gentleman. "Sit down here beside me, and we'll discuss the matter, or better still, let us walk up and down; it gets so chilly out on the hillside at this hour of evening."

And indeed it was more than chilly. The mist had started to rise. Already it roped the boles of the trees, and if it weren't for the little gentleman's company Packy would have been scared. As it was, he set about matching

his pace to the pace of his friend, and stepped
out boldly.

"I suppose you're a County Councillor, sir?"
he asked, as they paced along.

"Eh? A County Councillor? What's that?"
said the little man, and he stopped short in
his stride, but the next minute he started off
again. "Don't let us delay," he said. "It's
mortally cold out here."

So he wasn't a County Councillor? He didn't
even know what a Councillor was! Packy's
heart sank. Where did he come from at all?
And was it all for nothing he'd lost his time
and his firewood. It was very tiring too,
striding up and down on the top of the hill,
because at every minute the little gentleman
stepped out faster and faster, and where at
first, when they passed them, the windflowers
had shone out, each single as a star, now they
streamed past like ribbons of mist. Even the
little man was out of breath. He was panting
like the pinkeens that Packy and the
Tubridys caught in the Boyne and put into
jam-jars where they swam to the sides of the
glass, their mouths gaping. Chancing to
glance at him it seemed to Packy that his
companion had got a lot older looking. His
eyes looked very old.

"What's the matter, Packy?" asked the little man, just then, seeing him stare.

"Nothing, sir," said Packy—"I was just wondering if it is a thing that you are a foreigner?"

"Is it me?" cried the gentleman, "a foreigner!" He stopped short in astonishment. "I've been in this country a lot longer than you, Packy." He paused, "—about five thousand years longer, I should say."

Packy too stopped short.

Was the little man cracked, he wondered? This, however, was a point he could not very well ask him to settle. He would have to decide for himself. So he said nothing. But he wasn't going to pace up and down the hill any more.

"I think I'd better be going home, sir," he said politely, but decisively.

"Oh, but you can't go back to that wretched cottage. Not till I see if I can do something for you!" he cried. "Have you forgotten?"

Of course he hadn't forgotten. But if the gentleman was cracked, what use was there placing any hope in him?

"I've been thinking of your problem for some time past, Packy, as it happens," he said, "and it seems to me that there is very

little use in trying to do anything to that old
place of yours—"

That was sane enough, thought Packy.

"—and so," he went on, "what I have in
mind is that you come and live with *me*."

So he *was* cracked after all. Packy drew
back. But the little man went on eagerly. "I
live right near here—yes—just down there—
only a few paces," he cried, pointing down the
side of the hill towards the water's edge.

Now Packy wouldn't swear that he knew
every single step of the ground at this point,
because a great deal of it was covered with
briar and scrub, but he'd be prepared to
swear that there wasn't a house the size of a
sixpence on the side of that hill.

"I see you don't believe me." said the little
man. "Well—come and I'll show you."

Now, the little man was so insistent, and
Packy himself was so curious, that when the
former set off down the slope, Packy set off
after him, although it was by no means easy
to follow him, for the undergrowth was dense,
and the branches of the trees, that had never
been cut back, or broken by cattle, hung down
so low that in some places they touched the
ground. To pass under them Packy had
almost to go down on his knees. But the little

fellow knew his way like a rabbit. He looped
under the heavy boughs as easily as a bird,
while Packy stumbled after, as often as not
forgetting to lower his head, and getting a
crack on the pate. "Ouch!" he cried on one of
these occasions.

"What's up?" asked the little man, looking
irritably over his shoulder.

"I hit my head against a branch; that's all,"
said Packy.

The little man looked crossly at him.

"That wasn't a branch you hit against," he
said sharply, "it was a root."

And indeed he was right. At that point, the
hill sloped so steeply that the rain had washed
the clay from the roots of the trees till you could
walk under them in the same way as you'd walk
through the eye of a bridge. It was just as he
was about to duck under another of these big
branching roots after the little man, that Packy
noticed how dark it was on the other side, as if
something had come up between them and the
sky. He came to an abrupt stand. The little man,
on the other hand, darted into the dimness.

"Mind your step there," he cried, looking
back over his shoulder. "It's a bit dark, but
you'll get used to it." He fully expected Packy to
follow him.

But Packy stuck his feet in the ground.

"Hold on a minute, sir," he said. "If it's a cave you live in, I'm not going a step further."

He hadn't forgotten how, once, an uncle of his had come home from America, and hired a car and taken him and his mother to Newgrange to see the prehistoric caves. His mother couldn't be got to go into them, but he and his uncle crawled down a stone passage that was slimy and wet, and when they got to the caves they hardly had room to stand up. They could barely breathe either the air was so damp. And it had a smell like the smell that rises from a newly-made grave. All the time Packy kept thinking the earth would press down on the cave and crack it like an egg—and them along with it. No thank you! He had seen enough caves.

"You're not going to get me into any cave," he said stoutly. The little man ran out into the light again.

"It's not a cave," he cried. "Do you think we had to scratch holes for ourselves like badgers or foxes? We may live inside the hill but we move around under the earth the same way that you move around over it. You've a lot to learn yet, Packy, you and your generation."

"Is that so?" said Packy. "Well, we can move

in the air. And under the sea."

"Bah!" said the little man. "Not the way I meant! Not like the birds. Not like the fishes."

"I suppose you're right there," said Packy, but half-heartedly.

"What do you mean by supposing everything?" said the old man crossly. "Don't you ever say yes or no? I hope you haven't a suspicious streak in you? Perhaps I should have known that when you kept running home all the week every time I tried to get your attention."

"Oh, but that was different, sir," said Packy. "I thought then that you were one of the Shee."

At this, however, the little man began to laugh.

"And who in the name of the Sod do you think I am _now_?" he said.

"I don't know, sir," said Packy, "but I'm not afraid of you anyway—a nice kind gentleman like you—why should I?"

"And if I were to tell you that I _am_ one of the Shee," said the little man, "what would happen then?"

Packy pondered this.

"Perhaps you'd be only joking?" he said, but a doubtful look had come on his face.

"And if I wasn't joking," said the little man, "what then?"

"Well, sir," said Packy, "I suppose I'd be twice as glad then that I didn't go into the cave with you."

"I tell you it's *not* a cave!" screamed the little man. "And by the same token, will you stop calling us the Shee! What do they teach you in school at all, at all? Did you never hear tell of the Tuatha de Danaan? the noblest race that ever set foot in this isle? In five thousand years, no race has equalled us in skill or knowledge."

Five thousand years! Packy started. Had he heard aright?

"Excuse me, sir," he said then. "Are you alive or dead?"

It seemed quite a natural question to ask, but it angered the little man.

"Do I look as if I was dead?" he cried. "Wouldn't I be dust and ashes long ago if so?"

"Oh, I don't know about that," said Packy. "When my uncle hired the car that time—the time we went to Newgrange—we passed through Drogheda, and we went into the Cathedral to see Blessed Oliver Plunkett's head. It's in a box on the altar. He's been dead hundreds of years: and he's not dust and ashes!"

But truth to tell, there was a big difference between the little gentleman's head, and the head of the saint, because the venerable bishop's head looked like an old football, nothing more, while the little gentleman looked very much alive, especially at that moment, because he was leaping with anger.

"Are you taught nothing at all nowadays?" he cried in disgust. "Do you not know anything about the history of your country? Were you not taught that when we went into the hills we took with us the secret that mankind has been seeking ever since—the secret of eternal youth? But come! that's not the point. The point is—are you coming any further, or are you not?"

Now there was no doubt about it, the situation had changed. Packy stared past the little man, and although he could see nothing, his curiosity undecided him. What a story he'd have for the Tubridys if he'd once been inside that hill!

"Will you bring me back again, sir?" he asked, having in mind the story about the changelings.

The little man looked at him.

"Well, Packy, I may as well be straight with you. An odd time—now and again only—we take a notion for a human child and try to lure him away to live with us forever under the hills, but we always look for one who is dissatisfied with his lot in the world."

"Oh, but I'm not dissatisfied with my lot," cried Packy apprehensively.

"Oh come now!" said the little man, "didn't I often overhear you and your mother complaining about that wretched cottage of yours?"

"Oh, you might have heard us talking, sir, but it was my mother that was discontented: not me. I was only agreeing to keep her in good humour."

"What's that?" said the little man sharply. "Don't tell me I've got the wrong end of the stick. Are you sure of what you're saying, Packy? Because if that's the case I may as well stop wasting my time." He scowled very fiercely. After a minute though he seemed to remember his manners. "It's too bad," he said, "because you're the sort of lad I like."

"Thank you, sir," said Packy. "My mother will be pleased to hear that." Then as he made a move to go, upon an impulse he stopped. "I wonder, sir, if you'd mind my asking you a question before I go?"

"Why certainly not," said the little man.

"But be quick, boy; it's very cold out here on the hillside."

"Well, sir," said Packy, "I'd like to know if it's true about Marty Tubridy—I mean, is he a changeling, sir?"

"Is it Marty Tubridy? Of course not," said the old man. "Your mother was right there," he conceded. "We have no use for weedy little creatures like the Tubridys: it isn't everyone we fancy, I can tell you."

That was very gratifying to hear. His mother would be pleased at that too, thought Packy. Then he remembered that she would probably say it was all a likely story. He sighed.

The little man looked keenly at him.

"Are you changing your mind?"

Packy said nothing for a minute. Then he looked up.

"You didn't tell me whether I'd be able to get out again?" he asked.

"Really, Packy, you are an obstinate boy. I have no choice but to tell you the truth, which is that at the start I had no notion of letting you out again if I once got you inside, but as it's getting late, and I'm getting sick and tired arguing, I'm willing to make a bargain with you. I won't stop you from going home—if you

want to go yourself, but don't blame me if you
don't want to go!"

Well, that seemed fair enough.

"Oh, there's no fear of me wanting to stay,"
he said confidently. "Thank you kindly for
asking me, sir. I'll go on for a short while. But
wait a second while I take off my boots so I
won't dirty the place: my feet are shocking
muddy after slithering down that slope."

For a minute the little gentleman looked
oddly at him.

"Leave on your boots, Packy," he said; then
slowly and solemnly: "Don't leave anything
belonging to you outside. That's the very
thing I'd have made you do, if I was not going
to let you out again. I'd have had you leave
some part of your clothing—your cap, or your
scarf, or something, here on the outside of the
hill—like a man would leave his clothes on
the bank of the river if he was going to drown
himself—so that people would find them and
give up hopes of you. Because as long as
there's anyone outside in the world still
hoping a child will come back to them, it's
nearly as hard for us to keep him inside as if
he himself was still hoping to go back. Keep
your boots on your feet, boy. You can't say I'm
not being honest with you, can you?"

"I cannot, sir," said Packy, "but tell me, sir, those children you were telling me about—the ones that didn't want to go back to the world, did they always leave their shoes outside?"

"They did," said the little man.

"Did they now?" said Packy reflectively. "Wasn't that very foolish of them? How did they know they wouldn't be sorry when they got inside?"

The little man shrugged his shoulders.

"Ah sure don't we all have to take a chance some time or another in our lives?" he said. "Look at us! Before we came to Erin we were endlessly sailing the seas looking for a land to our liking. And many a one we found. But it never satisfied us for long. No matter how often we beached our boats, we soon set sail again, till one day we saw *this* island rise up out of the seas and we put all our trust in the promise of her emerald shores. Before we went a foot inland do you know what we did? We set fire to our boats, down on the grey sands! That was taking a chance, wasn't it? So you can't expect me to have much sympathy with people that won't take a chance with their boots! Have you made up your mind about yours, by the way? You won't leave them? Very well then, lace them up again on you, and don't mind them being muddy. I'll get one of the women inside to give them a rub of a blacking brush. They're very muddy all right. Never mind that now though—follow me!' Then he turned around and ducking under the root of the tree again, he walked into what seemed to Packy to be a solid wall of earth.

But just as fog shrinks from light, or frost from fire, so, as they went inward, the earth seemed to give way before them. Nor was it the cold wet rock of Newgrange either, but a warm dry clay in which, Packy noticed with interest as they went along, there were different layers of clay and sand and gravel and stone, just like he had seen in Swainstown Quarry when he went there once on a tipper-lorry. In fact he was so interested in the walls of clay that he hardly realized how deep into the hill they were going until the little man came to a stop.

"Well! Here we are!" he said, and Packy saw that they had arrived at what at first seemed to be a large room, but which he soon saw was merely a large space made by several people all gathered together.

But apparently these people rarely moved very far from where they were, for around them they had collected a variety of articles that suggested permanent habitation, in the way that furniture suggests habitation in a house. Not that the articles in the cave were furniture in any real sense of the word. Tables and chairs there were none. But in a corner a big harp gleamed, and randomly around about were strewn a number of vessels, basins and ewers and yes, a row of gleaming milking pails! With astonishment, Packy noticed that all these vessels, and the harp too, were as bright as if they were made of gold! He was staring at them when the little man shook him by the arm.

"Well, how do you like it down here?" he cried, and he was so feverishly excited he was dancing about on the tips of his toes.

Now, Packy didn't want to be rude, but the fact of the matter was that only for the gold basins and the gold pails, and the big gold harp, he didn't see anything very wonderful about the place. But of course, they would be something to tell the Tubridys about.

"They're not real gold, sure they're not?" he asked.

"Of course they are gold," said the little man. And then, seeing that Packy seemed to doubt him, he frowned. "In our day Ireland was the Eldorado of the world. I thought

everyone knew that! Everything was made of
gold. Even our buttons! Even the latchets of
our shoes!" And he held out his foot to show
that, sure enough, although Packy hadn't
noticed it before, the latchets were solid gold.
"It was a good job for us that gold was
plentiful," he said irritably. "I don't know
what we'd do if we had to put up with some of
the utensils you have today."

"Oh, they're not too bad," said Packy.
"There are grand enamel pails and basins in
Leonards of Trim!"

"Is that so?" said the little man coldly.
"Perhaps it's a matter of taste. To be candid
with you though, Packy, I wouldn't like to
have to spend five thousand years looking at
some of the delph on your kitchen-dresser."

Packy laughed. "There'd be no fear you'd
have to look that long at them," he said.
"They don't last any time. They's always
getting broken."

"Ah, that's not the way in here," said the
little man. "Nothing ever gets cracked down
here; nothing ever gets broken."

Packy stared. "You don't tell me!" he said.
"Do you never knock the handle off a cup, or a
jug?" That was a thing he was always doing.

The little man shook his head.

"Oh, but I forgot," said Packy, "gold wouldn't break so easily." Not that he thought it was such a good idea to have cups made of gold. When you'd pour your tea into them, wouldn't it get so hot it would scald the lip off you?"

One day in the summer that was gone past, he and the Tubridys went fishing on the Boyne up beyond Rathnally, and they took a few grains of tea with them in case they got dry. They forgot to bring cups though, and they had to empty out their tin-cans of worms and use them for cups. But the metal rim of the can got red hot the minute the tea went into it, and they couldn't drink a drop. Gold would be just the same.

But in fact, there were no cups at all, it appeared.

"One no longer has any need for food, Packy," said the little man, "once one has learned the secret of eternal youth."

"Do you mean you don't eat anything?" cried Packy, "anything at all? Don't you ever feel hungry?"

"No, child," said the little man sedately. "Desire withers when perfection flowers. And if you stay here with us for long, you'll lose all desire too."

"You're joking, sir!" said Packy, doubtful. At

that very minute he had a powerful longing for a cut of bread and a swig of milk. Indeed he glanced involuntarily at the gold milking pails. The Tubridys said the Shee often stole into byres and stripped the cows' udders.

The little man had seen his glance and must have read his thoughts.

"A little harmless fun now and then," he said, shamefacedly.

Had they been stripping cows lately? Packy wondered. Perhaps there might be a dreg in the bottom of one of the buckets? He craned his neck to see into them. They were all empty!

"I'm very dry, sir," he said.

"That's only your imagination," said the little man crossly. "Stand there for a minute, like a good boy," he said then, and he darted over to one of the women. "There's something wrong somewhere," he said to a woman that was sitting by the harp. And then he snapped his fingers. "It's the boots," he cried.

The young woman stood up. "Give me your boots, son," she said, "and I'll get the mud off them."

Now Packy was always shy of strange women, but this one spoke so like Mrs Tubridy that he felt at home with her at once. And indeed, just as Mrs Tubridy would have done, she caught the sleeve of his coat in her two fists and began to rub off the mud that was caked on it. It didn't brush off so easily though.

"I'll have to take a brush to it," she said. "Take your coat off, son, and I'll give it a rub too when I'm doing your boots."

"That's very kind of you, ma'am," said Packy, and he took off his coat. It was the coat of his good suit. His mother made him wear it that day so she'd get a chance to put a patch on the elbow of his old one. Under his coat he was wearing his old jumper.

"Is there mud on your jumper as well?" asked the young woman.

"Oh no, ma'am," said Packy. "That's only splatters of pig-food and chicken-mash."

"What matter! Give it to me!" she said. "I may as well make the one job of it."

But when he took off his jumper his shirt was a show.

"That's only sweat-marks," he protested, knowing she'd proffer to do the shirt as well. But there was no holding back from her any more than from his mother.

"Here, sonny," she cried. "Go behind that harp over there and take every stitch off you and we'll get them all cleaned and pressed for you. You can put this on while you're waiting," she said, and she whipped a green dust-sheet off another harp.

It seemed to Packy that such courtesy was hardly necessary, but he went obediently behind the harp and stripped to the skin. Just as he reached out his hand, however, for the dust-sheet, the young woman came back with a big gold basin of water.

"What's that for?" cried Packy, drawing away from her.

She shoved a towel into his hands.

"Wrap that towel around you," she said, "while I try to get some of the dirt off you before you get back into your clean clothes."

"Mud isn't dirt!" cried Packy indignantly. "My mother washes me every Saturday night," he cried, "and this is only Tuesday."

At this point the little man hurried over to them.

"It's not a question of cleanliness, Packy," he said. "It's a question of hospitality. Surely the ancient customs of the Gael have not fallen into such disuse in Ireland today? Does your mother not offer ablutions to those who cross your threshold?"

"What's that, sir?" said Packy, but he recollected that one day when his teacher called at the cottage, he slipped on the spud-stone at the gate and fell into a puddle, and that day his mother ran into the house and got out a big enamel basin and filled it with water for him to wash his hands. Then she got a towel and wiped the mud off the tail of his coat. She offered him an old pair of his father's pants too, but he wouldn't put them on. Oh, his mother wasn't far behind anyone, he thought, when it came to hospitality. And so, to show that he was very familiar with all such rites, he made an opening in the towel, and unbared first one hand, and then the other.

"That's a good boy," she said. "Now your foot. Now the other one!"

She didn't stop at his feet though, and before he knew where he was, there wasn't a cranny of him she hadn't scrubbed.

Never in his life had he been washed like that. It reminded him of the way Mrs Tubridy scoured old grandpa Tubridy's corpse the night he was waked.

He was especially struck with the way the black rims of his nails stood out against his bone-white hands. And he greatly regretted it when the young woman prised out the dirt with a little gold pin. And when she was done with his finger-nails, she began to prod at his toe-nails.

They must be terrible clean people altogether, he thought. His own mother was supposed to be the cleanest woman in the parish, yet she'd never dream of going that far. When his father died, and she was describing the kind of mortuary card she wanted to get for him, she held up her hand to the shopkeeper and showed him the rim of dirt under her nail.

"I want the border of the card as deep as that!" she said. Indeed she'd speak of the black of her nail as readily as another person would speak of the white of his eye!

These people must be terrible particular people, he thought. All those gold basins and gold ewers were for washing themselves, he supposed. And just then the young woman took out a comb and began to rake his hair so hard he felt like as if he'd been sculled. But the comb was solid gold too.

"Oh wait till the Tubridys hear about this," he said ecstatically.

The young woman looked at him in a very peculiar way, and then she looked at the little man.

"There's something wrong still," said the little man.

"Are you sure you washed every nook of him?" he asked. He'd got very cross again.

"I did," said the young woman, and she was cross too.

I hope they're not going to start fighting, while I'm standing here in my skin, thought Packy, and he shivered. He ventured to pluck the little man by the sleeve.

"Excuse me, sir," he said as politely as possible. "Are my own clothes near ready do you think?"

But these innocent words seemed to infuriate the little man, and he turned on the young woman again.

"You missed some part of him!" he shouted. "What about his ears? Did you take the wax out of them?"

"Oh, I forgot," cried the young woman, and whipping the gold pin out of her bodice again she began to root in his ears.

There was such a lot of wax in his ears, Packy was shamed and he thought he'd better pass it off with a joke.

"I'll have no excuse now but to get up when my mother calls me in the morning," he said.

But the little man seemed ready to dance with rage at that. "What about his teeth?" he cried, ignoring him and calling to the young woman. "Maybe there's a bit of food stuck between them?"

"That's it surely!" cried the young woman. "Open your mouth, Packy," she said, and she began to poke between his teeth with the needle, but to no avail. There was not a thing between his bright white teeth.

He had to laugh. "That's the way the vet opens Bessie's mouth," he said. "Bessie is our cow."

"Bother your cow Bessie," said the little man, and he caught the young woman by the arm and shook her. "Could there be a bit of grit in his eye?"

"I don't think so," said the young woman, "but we can try." And she reached out and pushed up his eyelid. "Nothing there," she said. Then she looked into his other eye. "Nothing there either."

What was all this about? Packy wondered. What were they looking to find? And what about the milk? He thought they were going to try to get him a cup of milk after they'd washed him. He was still thirsty. But it was hardly worth while troubling them to get it for him, because he'd have to be going home. It would be getting very dark in the woods outside, he thought, and he looked around.

"Have you no windows?" he cried.

"What would we want with windows!" the little man exclaimed. "If some people like to wake up and find the quilt all wet with rain, there are other people who don't," he said venomously.

"Oh, but it isn't always raining," cried Packy, knowing it was his own little window at home to which the little man was referring. And thinking of that small square window on a sunny morning his face lit up. There was something to be said for a broken pane at times. "Once a swallow flew in my window—through the hole in the glass," he said, and he gave a laugh of delight at the memory of it.

But the young woman made a face.

"Don't talk about birds!" she said. "Dirty little things, always letting their droppings fall on everything."

"It's great manure, though," cried Packy. "If you could get enough of it, you could make your fortune selling it to the people in the towns."

At this however the little man shuddered violently.

"We may at times have vague regrets for the world outside, Packy," he said in an admonitory tone, "regrets for the stars, and the flowers, and the soft summer breezes, but we are certainly not sorry to have said farewell to the grosser side of life to which you have just now—somewhat indelicately— alluded."

Packy stared, and there was a puzzled look on his face but suddenly it cleared and he nodded his head sagaciously. "I suppose you were born in the town, sir?" he said. "My mother says when people from the towns come out for a day in the country, they never stop talking about the smell of the flowers and the smell of the hay, but give them one smell of a cow shed and they're ready to run back to the town. But it's not a bad smell at all when you're used to it. I suppose it makes a difference too when you have a cow of your own; like us. I love the smell of the dung in Bessie's byre."

"Indeed?" said the little man. "You don't tell me!" He must have been sarcastic though, because he turned to the young woman. "That's the limit!" he said. "I think we may give him up as a bad job." He turned back to Packy. "Do you still feel the need of a cup of milk?"

"If it's not too much trouble, sir, please," said Packy.

"I didn't say you were going to get it," said the little man testily. "I asked if you felt the need of it."

"I do, sir," said Packy, "but perhaps it's not worth while bothering you. I ought to be thinking of getting home."

"Did you hear that?" the little man cried, fairly screeching, as he turned to the young woman. "Oh, there is no doubt about it, there is something wrong somewhere. We'd better let him go home."

The young woman looked very sour. "The sooner the better, if you ask me," she said. "What kind of a child is he at all? Why didn't you pick an ordinary one?"

"But he *is* an ordinary child," screamed the little man. "It's not my fault, and it's certainly not his!" He turned to Packy. "Don't mind her, Packy. Women are all the same, under the hills, or over the hills. You may as well go home. And you'd be advised to start off soon, because it will be dark out on the hillside. Wait a minute till I get your clothes!"

When they got the clothes, Packy couldn't help noticing that the mud was still on them. And his boots were still in a shocking state.

"Tch, tch, tch!" said the little man. "Women again! Try to overlook it, Packy, as a favour to me. —Well? Are you ready? Better take my hand: it's always easier to get in here than it is to get out!"

Yet a second later Packy saw a chink of light ahead, and it widened and widened until suddenly he was at the opening of the hill again, and above him was a great expanse of moonlit sky.

"I'm afraid there was a shower while we were inside," said the little man. "I hope your twigs didn't get wet!"

"Oh, I may leave them till morning anyway," said Packy. He had been wondering how he'd carry them the way his finger had begun to throb with the pain of the thorn in it.

"And why would you do that?" said the little man. "Won't your mother want them first thing in the morning?"

"She will," said Packy, " —but my finger is beginning to beal, I'm afraid," and he stuck it into his mouth again.

"What is the matter with it?" cried the little man. "Show me!"

"Oh, it's nothing, sir," said Packy. "Only an old thorn I got when I snatched up a bit of blackthorn by mistake. It's no good for kindling."

But the little man was beside himself.

"Show me! Show me!" he screeched. "A thorn!" and he caught Packy's hand and tried to peer at it, but the moon had gone behind a cloud. He stamped his foot angrily. "You don't mean to tell me it was there all the time! Oh, weren't we blind! It was *that* thorn kept pulling your mind back to the world. Oh, how was it we didn't see it?"

"How could you see it, sir?" said Packy. "It's gone in deep. It'll have to have a poultice put on it."

At that moment the moon sailed into a clearing in the clouds and shone down bright. The little man caught him by the sleeve.

"Will you come back for a minute and we'll take it out for you?" he cried. "There's nothing safer than a gold pin when probing for a thorn."

Packy held back. The little man meant well, he supposed, but God help him if he was depending on that same young woman who was supposed to have polished his boots and brushed his suit.

"I'd better go home and get my mother to do it," he said.

The little man let go of his sleeve.

"All right, Packy," he said. "Go home to your mother. I can't blame you. I suppose you saw through the whole thing anyway! As long as there was any particle of the earth still on you, you'd never lose your hankering for home. But I hope those women didn't handle you too roughly."

"Oh not at all, sir," said Packy politely.

His mother wouldn't have to wash him again for a year of Saturdays.

"Well I'm glad to think you bear no ill will," said the little man. "I wouldn't like you to have any hard feelings towards us." Then he shook his head sadly. "You must admit it was a bit unfortunate for me to be bested by a bit of a thorn. Ah well, it can't be helped now."

He looked so sad Packy felt sad too.

"I suppose I'll see you around the woods some time, sir," he said.

But the little man shook his head from side to side.

"I don't think you will," he said.

There seemed no more to say.

"Well, I suppose I'd better be going," said Packy. "I hope I'll find my way."

"Oh, you'll find your way all right," said the little man. "The moon is a fine big May moon. I'm sorry about your boots," he added, calling after him, but he couldn't resist a last sly dig. "Anyway you'd only destroy them again going in through the puddles around your door!"

"Oh, I don't mind the puddles," said Packy. "Only for the puddles we couldn't keep ducks; they'd be always straying down to the Boyne, and in the end they'd swim away from us altogether. Puddles have their uses."

At that the little man laughed.

"I never met the like of you, Packy!" he said. "Good-bye!"

"Good-bye sir," said Packy.

And then he was alone.

Slowly he started up the hill until he came to the top where the windflowers were all closed up for the night. But on their shiny leaves the moon lay white. And there, a dark patch in the middle of the glade, was his bundle of twigs.

He gathered them up. His finger was still throbbing but he paid no heed to the pain. Only for that thorn he might never have got out of the cave. Because it wasn't much better than a cave, no matter what the little man said about it. He began to whistle. And when he came to the pathway leading to the gap in the demesne wall he ran down it full-tilt. In a minute he was out on the road again.

There had been a shower all right. All along the road there were puddles. But in every puddle there was a star. And when he got to the cottage the puddles around the door were as big as ever, but in them shone the whole glory of the heavens.

"Is that you, Packy?" cried the widow, running out to the door in a terrible state. "What kept you so late, son?"

"Oh, wait till I tell you," cried Packy, although he knew right well what she'd say:

A likely story!

Published by Poolbeg

The King of Ireland's Son

by

Brendan Behan

Illustrated by PJ Lynch

The King of Ireland sends his three sons to discover the source of the heavenly music that can be heard throughout his kingdom. The youngest prince finds a beautiful maiden held captive by a fierce giant and forced to make music all day long. To defeat the giant he calls on the help of a magical stallion . . .

Brendan Behan's spirited retelling of the traditional tale of *The King of Ireland's Son* is full of incident and humour. The rich imagery of the story has inspired artist PJ Lynch to create some of his most stunning work to date.

ISBN: 1-85371-622-7

Published by Poolbeg

The Queen of Aran's Daughter

by

Maura Laverty

Her skin was the colour of an old brogue, and her body was as twisted as the branches of a hawthorn tree that has been beaten out of shape by the wind. She had hair as coarse and as straight as a cow's tail, and the few teeth she had in her mouth were crooked and yellow.

So begins *The Queen of Aran's Daughter*, a collection of seven original fairy tales by Maura Laverty. Set in the west of Ireland these island tales tell of a time of Kings and Queens, princes and princesses and talking animals – and everywhere the fairy folk. It is a place where happy events are really celebrated, where parties last seven days and seven nights. It is a world of simple values where "a kind heart is more powerful that any magic."

ISBN: 1-85371-711-8